Little Grey Rabbit's Party

by Alison Uttley

Pictures by Margaret Tempest

COLLINS COLOUR CUBS

One evening Hare came racing down the lane to the little house at the end of the wood. He dashed into the kitchen where Squirrel and Grey Rabbit sat.

"I took a short cut across the lawn of the farmhouse," said he, "and I heard a strange noise."

"Oh? What was it Hare?" asked Squirrel, looking up from her knitting.

"It was a party!" said Hare. "I stood up on tiptoe by the juniper bush, and I looked through the window. I saw lots of little boys and girls bobbing up and down, and playing games and singing."

"Are they there now?" cried Squirrel, throwing her knitting on the floor.

"Yes. I hurried home to tell you both. I raced like the North wind."

Grey Rabbit sat very still, her eyes open wide as she heard Hare's tale.

"Let's go and watch them," cried Squirrel. "We've never seen a party."

They dragged on their wraps and mufflers and were ready in less than a minute. Grey Rabbit put a fire-guard round the fire, Squirrel locked the door, and put the key under a stone. Hare jumped up and down crying, "Hurry up! Hurry up! You'll be too late."

He raced along with great leaps, and Squirrel and Grey Rabbit hastened after him.

Down the fields they ran, along the lanes, and under the gate. They ran across the lawn and stood under the juniper bush, staring at the darkened house.

"I can't see anything," murmured Grey Rabbit.

"Nor I," muttered Squirrel.

"They've shuttered the windows," cried Hare, disappointedly.

Little sounds of merriment and cries of joy came from the hidden room.

Hare walked slowly round the corner and the others trailed after.

Then Hare gave a shrill cry. "Here's a little window they've forgotten. Come and look here!"

Hare stood on tiptoes, Squirrel climbed a rose bush and Grey Rabbit scrambled on top of a wheelbarrow.

In the warm, bright room they could see little boys and girls playing Blind Man's Buff, and Hunt the Thimble, and Musical Chairs.

Then the children trooped into another room, and they saw no more.

"What do you think of that?" said Hare. "It was my discovery!"

"It was very clever of you," said Squirrel, but little Grey Rabbit said nothing.

"Why don't you speak, Grey Rabbit?" cried Hare. "Didn't you like it?"

"Yes," whispered Grey Rabbit. "I was just thinking and wondering and wishing. That's all."

Hare dashed off and reached home first. "Do let's have supper," said he. "That party made me hungry." So Grey Rabbit filled bowls with bread and milk, and they all sat round the table.

"Couldn't we give a party?" asked Hare.

"Why not?" said Squirrel.

"That's just what I was thinking about," said Grey Rabbit, "but I don't know much about such things."

Hare reached down his riddle book, but there was nothing about parties.

"You had better ask Wise Owl," said Squirrel. "He knows everything."

Grey Rabbit went pale. "I don't mind very much about a party," she said.

"Oh, do! He won't hurt you. You're a favourite of his," they both cried.

So the next day Grey Rabbit went off with a pot of crab-apple jelly in her basket.

She ran through the wood and rang the little silver bell beside Wise Owl's neat small door.

Wise Owl put his head out.

"Who's there?" he said, fiercely. And then he recognised Grey Rabbit, and said more gently, "What do you want?"

"If you please, Wise Owl," she said, "we want to give a party and we don't know how. Can you tell us?"

"It's a long time since I was at a party," said Wise Owl. "But have you brought your present?"

Grey Rabbit held up the pot of crab-apple jelly, and Owl with a "Humph" of approval ate it all up.

He went back into his tree and Grey Rabbit sat waiting and wondering, when the door opened and Owl tossed down a little red book. "How to give a party" it was called.

"Don't thank me," he grunted, "but remember to send an invitation."

Hare and Squirrel seized the book as soon as Grey Rabbit arrived home, and buried their noses in it.

"Turn the Trencher, Blind Man's Buff, Hunt the Thimble," they read.

"Come and explain all this to us, Grey Rabbit," they said.

Little Grey Rabbit sat by the fire and read the party book and Squirrel and Hare sat either side, and listened.

There were Forfeits and Invitations and Thimbles, R.S.V.P. and Iced Cake to remember.

"What's R.S.V.P.?" asked Hare.

"Rat Shan't Visit Party," replied Grey Rabbit.

"What is Forfeits?" he asked.

"Cry in one corner, sing in another, dance in another, and laugh in another," read Grey Rabbit.

"I'll take charge of Turn the Trencher," said Hare. "Mole has a silver crown which will make a grand trencher. He'll lend it to me when he hears about the party."

"I hope my thimble won't get lost in Hide the Thimble," said Grey Rabbit. "There isn't another in all the fields and woods."

The preparations began. Grey Rabbit went shopping and came back with caraway seeds, candied peel, beech-nut flour, and cinnamon sticks. Squirrel looked in the woods and found hoards of nuts which she ground in a bowl. Hare brought a basket of eggs from the Speckledy Hen.

Every morning Hare learned his forfeits as though they were lessons. "Cry in one corner, laugh in another, sing in another and dance in another," he repeated.

He ran over the fields and knocked at Mole's back door.

Mole put his head out and asked, "What's the matter, Hare?"

"I want to borrow that big silver coin of yours," answered Hare.

"Certainly," replied Mole, and he trundled it to the door. "What do you want it for, Hare?"

"It's a secret," said Hare. "But I'll tell you. We're giving a party, and this is for Turn the Trencher. You are coming. There are forfeits – Sing in one corner, sit in another, go to sleep in another. No, that's wrong. I must ask Grey Rabbit."

"Stop a minute," cried Mole. "Tell me slowly."

"No. It's a secret," said Hare. "Good-bye till Party Day."

Away he went, rolling the silver coin towards home. On the way back he met little Fuzzypeg, coming home from school.

"Are you bowling a hoop?" asked Fuzzypeg.

"No, this is for Turn the Trencher," explained Hare. "We're giving a party, and you are invited. But it's a secret." Hare put his paw over his mouth.

"Oh," cried Fuzzypeg. "Tell me more."

"No, it's a secret," whispered Hare, and he ran on.

By the time he reached home, he had told the secret to so many that all over the fields and woods and lanes the news spread that Hare was having a party, and there would be forfeits for tea.

Each day Grey Rabbit baked and brewed, and Squirrel and Hare collected sticks to make a big fire to cook all the dainties.

Little Grey Rabbit wrote the invitations on sparkling holly leaves.

She gave the bundle of letters to Robin and asked him to deliver them. "Take one to Moldy Warp, three to the Hedgehog family, one to Wise Owl and several to the Brown Rabbits and Squirrels.

"But I invited the Cows and Horses, the Pigs and Geese and Hens," said Hare.

"Oh Hare!" she gasped. "You must tell them it was a mistake. How could we fit them in?"

"I'll make it all right," said Robin. "I'm used to explaining." And he flew off.

The day of the party came. They all rose very early as there was still so much to do. Grey Rabbit decorated the room with red-berried holly and delicate white mistletoe.

Across the middle of the room was the tea table. There were pink cakes and white cakes, mince pies and sandwiches of potted cobnuts, and roasted chestnuts. In the middle was the party cake, covered with icing which Hare had brought from the top of the pond.

When the full moon peeped out from behind the trees, the three went upstairs to dress. Hare put on his best red coat. Squirrel wore her yellow dress. Little Grey Rabbit draped round her shoulders a pale scarf of fine cobwebs. On her feet she wore her silver birch slippers.

Grey Rabbit ran downstairs and took a last look round to see if all was ready.

Suddenly she heard a soft shuffle and thump, and she saw Rat's hungry eyes peering in.

"R.S.V.P." whispered Grey Rabbit, but she slipped outside with a mince pie and left it on a stone. Rat sidled up, snatched it and ran off.

Old Hedgehog arrived with a can of milk. "I've come right early," said he, "but I knew you wanted milk for the party."

There was a knock at the door and Mrs Hedgehog and Fuzzypeg hurried in. Mrs Hedgehog wore her best silk dress, and Fuzzypeg had new shoes that squeaked.

Mole, in black velvet, followed. He brought a box of blue beads, threaded on a hair of Duchess's tail, for Grey Rabbit. She thanked him and held their coldness to her cheek.

Then came a party of Brown Rabbits and the family of Squirrels. Water Rat followed, slim and handsome in his starched frills.

"But where's Wise Owl?" asked Hare.

"Owl? Is he coming?" Everyone looked nervous, and the youngest rabbit started for the door.

Little Grey Rabbit grabbed his paw. "It's quite safe," she said. "A party is a Truce. He's quite friendly here. You mustn't go. We'll start without him."

"We are going to begin with Blind Man's Buff," said Squirrel. "Come along, Hedgehog, and be blindfolded."

She tied the handkerchief over Hedgehog's eyes, twisted him three times round and sprang away. Hedgehog groped about the room, catching his prickles in Squirrel's dress and Grey Rabbit's cuff until at last he caught someone. But he guessed wrong and had to hunt again.

Next he caught Hare and it wasn't difficult to know who it was.

Hare, with the handkerchief over his eyes, leaped about the room, until suddenly he nearly fell over Mole who was caught.

Straightaway he caught Grey Rabbit and she pounced on the youngest rabbit:

There was a little sobbing noise under the table, and Grey Rabbit turned up the cloth. Fuzzypeg sat weeping into his new handkerchief. "Nobody's found me!" he wailed. "I'm nobody's nuffin!" So Grey Rabbit lifted him out and helped him to be found.

They all sat down to tea. Like snow in summer the cakes and buns and sandwiches faded away.

"Wise Owl has forgotten to come," said Hare, as he passed the mince pies. Grey Rabbit set a portion aside for her chief guest, lest he should be tempted to forget the Truce.

Hare cut the big cake and gave everyone his slice with a piece of cold snow and ice from the top.

"Turn the Trencher!" shouted Hare, jumping up from the table, as soon as he had finished.

They pushed the table back and sat in a circle on the floor. Hare spun the silver-white coin. "Fuzzypeg!" he called and the little hedgehog rushed to catch it before it fell.

"Little Grey Rabbit!" called Fuzzypeg, but she could not get there in time and the trencher fell.

"A forfeit," said Hare and Grey Rabbit gave him her white cuff.

Mole was slow too and he had to pay a forfeit.

When Hare had a collection of forfeits he stopped the game and hid his face in his paws.

"Here is a thing and a very pretty thing and what is the owner to do?" asked Grey Rabbit, holding up a red scarf.

"You must cry in one corner, laugh in another, dance in another and sing in another," said Hare, getting his jingle right.

Just as old Hedgehog was singing in a husky voice, "The lass that loved a milkman", the door was pushed open and Wise Owl stalked in.

In a twinkle, everyone had disappeared; under the table, behind the chairs, even in the grandfather clock. Only Grey Rabbit remained.

"Where's the party?" he asked. "Come out! Don't be afraid."

One by one they crawled out and the game continued while Owl ate his tea.

"Now we'll play Hunt the Thimble," said Grey Rabbit, and she brought out her tiny silver thimble.

"You hide it first, Wise Owl," said she, and they all bundled out of the room into the garden.

Owl looked here and he looked there, but he could not see a good place. He took the thimble in his beak, and swallowed it.

Then he called the others in, and of course they couldn't find it anywhere.

"We give up," they said.

"I've swallowed it," said Wise Owl. Little Grey Rabbit nearly cried.

"But I can't do my mending now," she faltered.

"But we can't play now," said Squirrel.

"We'll ask riddles instead," said Wise Owl. "What most resembles a Squirrel up a tree?"

When they all gave up, he said, "A Squirrel down a tree."

"How many sticks go to building a crow's nest?" asked Hare.

"None, because they are all carried," he gave the answer himself, triumphantly.

"What lives in winter, dies in summer, and grows with its root upwards?" asked Wise Owl. They all scratched their heads, but Hare knew. "An icicle," said he, and Wise Owl stared in astonishment. "I must go now," said he. "I have another engagement," and he waddled to the door.

"Thank you for a very pleasant evening," he said, and he flew up into the sky.

Hare mopped his brow and all the
animals jumped for joy.

"Let's end up with a dance," said Water Rat. So they danced the polka, and Hare played the jolly tune on his flute.

Then someone looked out at the moon which was sailing high in the sky. There was the Great Bear above, beaming down to light them home.

"Goodnight! Goodnight!" they said. "Thank you, Squirrel, Hare and Grey Rabbit for the most beautiful party."

Hare put his flute in its case and Squirrel and Grey Rabbit tidied away the crumbs from the feast. Then upstairs they all went to bed, yawning sleepily.

Little Grey Rabbit opened her attic window and held her blue beads up in the moonlight so that they shone like blue flames.

"Although I did lose my dear thimble, it was a most beautiful party," she whispered.

Only the bare trees and the twinkling
stars heard her.

Alison Uttley's original story has been
abridged for this book.

ISBN 0 00 194195 10
Text Copyright © John Uttley 1978
Illustrations Copyright © Margaret Tempest 1978
Printed in Great Britain